# A Sunny Day

First published in 2010
by Wayland

Text copyright © Cynthia Rider
Illustration copyright © Nicola Evans

Wayland
338 Euston Road
London NW1 3BH

Wayland Australia
Level 17/207 Kent Street
Sydney, NSW 2000

Series Editor: Louise John
Editor: Katie Powell
Cover design: Paul Cherrill
Design: D.R.ink
Consultant: Shirley Bickler

A CIP catalogue record for this book is available from the British Library.

ISBN 9780750260589

Printed in China

Wayland is a division of Hachette Children's Books,
an Hachette UK Company

www.hachette.co.uk

# A Sunny Day

Written by Cynthia Rider
Illustrated by Nicola Evans

WAYLAND

It's a sunny day.
Watch me swinging
on my swing.

It's a sunny day.
Watch me sliding
on my slide.

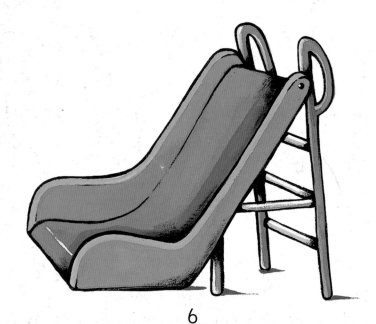

It's a sunny day.
Watch me jumping
on my trampoline.

It's a sunny day.
Watch me riding
on my bike.

It's a sunny day.
Watch me playing
in my tent.

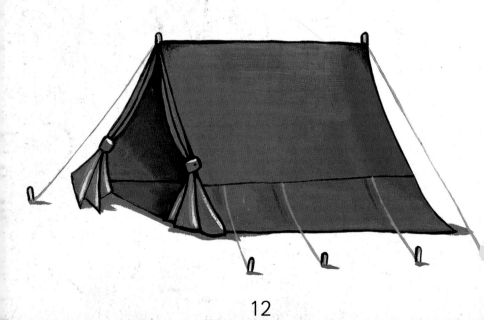

It's a sunny day.
Watch me climbing
in the tree.

It's a sunny day.
Watch me digging
in the sand.

It's a sunny day.
Watch me splashing
in my pool.

It's a sunny day.
Watch us playing
in the sun!

# Guiding a First Read of
# A Sunny Day

It is important to talk through the book with the child before they read it alone. This prepares them for the way the story unfolds, and allows them to enjoy the pictures as you both talk naturally, using the language they will later encounter when reading. Read them the brief overview, and then follow the suggestions below:

**1. Talking through the book**
**The two children are playing together out in the sun.**
**They are taking turns playing on the bike and the**
**slide and the trampoline, as the other child watches.**

The title of this book is: **A Sunny Day.**
Let's look at the pictures. On page 4,
the girl says, "It's a sunny day.
Watch me swinging on my swing."
Now let's see what the boy says on the next page.
Yes, "It's a sunny day. Watch me sliding
on my slide."

Continue through the book, guiding the discussion to fit the text as the child looks at the illustrations.

On page 16, the girl is digging in the sand.
So what does she say? And on the next page,
what does the boy say? On the last page, they
both say, "It's a sunny day. Watch us playing
in the sun!"

## 2. A first reading of the book

Ask the child to read the book independently, pointing carefully under each word (tracking), while thinking about the story. Praise attempts by the child to correct themselves, and prompt them to use their letter knowledge, the punctuation and check the meaning, for example:

**You said, "See me splashing in my pool".**
**Just check the words carefully again.**
**What sound does 'see' start with?**
**Would 'watch' fit? Read it again and check.**
**Well done.**

**That's a 'trampoline'. Now you try reading that word.**

## 3. Follow-up activities

The high frequency words in this title are:
**a   day   it's   me   my   on**

· Select a new high frequency word, and ask the child to find it throughout the book. Discuss the shape of the letters and the letter sounds.
· To memorise the word, ask the child to write it in the air, then write it repeatedly on a whiteboard or on paper, leaving a space between each attempt.

## 4. Encourage

· Reading the book again – with expression.
· Drawing a picture based on the story.
· Writing one or two sentences using the practised words.

**START READING** is a series of highly enjoyable books for beginner readers. **The books have been carefully graded to match the Book Bands widely used in schools.** This enables readers to be sure they choose books that match their own reading ability.

### Look out for the Band colour on the book in our Start Reading logo.

The Bands are:

Pink Band 1A & 1B

Red Band 2

Yellow Band 3

Blue Band 4

Green Band 5

Orange Band 6

Turquoise Band 7

Purple Band 8

Gold Band 9

**START READING** books can be read independently or shared with an adult. They promote the enjoyment of reading through satisfying stories supported by fun illustrations.

**Cynthia Rider** lives in the Peak District of Derbyshire and often finds inspiration for her stories in the countryside around her. She particularly enjoys writing for young children and encouraging their love of reading.

**Nicola Evans** works as a freelance illustrator in a small village on the south coast of England, where she lives with her husband and three-year-old daughter. She loves illustrating for children, helping to bring books alive with her characters and colours.